CHRIS

LIGHTHOUSE

Chris Binchy was born in 1970. His first novel, *The Very Man*, appeared in 2003 and was short-listed for the Irish Book of the Year Award, while his second novel, *People Like Us*, was published in 2004. He lives in Dublin.

NEW ISLAND *Open Door*

LIGHTHOUSE
First published 2008
by New Island
2 Brookside
Dundrum Road
Dublin 14

www.newisland.ie

A CIP catalogue record for this book is available from the British
Library.

ISBN 978-1-905494-81-1

New Island receives financial assistance from
The Arts Council (An Chomhairle Ealaíon), Dublin, Ireland.

Printed in Ireland by ColourBooks
Cover design by Artmark

1 3 5 4 2

Dear Reader,

On behalf of myself and the other contributing authors, I would like to welcome you to the sixth Open Door series. We hope that you enjoy the books and that reading becomes a lasting pleasure in your life.

Warmest wishes,

Patricia Scanlan.

Patricia Scanlan
Series Editor

One

It is bright when I wake up. I worry that I am too late and that she will have gone already. But when I sit up and look out, I see that the light is wrong. Still too orange and low. I go to the bathroom and pee. It is six o'clock. On the landing I can hear her breathing from their bedroom. Her breath is heavy in one direction only. Back in my room I lie on the bed, my head resting on my arms, watching out the window. It is only an hour and a half to wait, but

I feel myself start to drift. I dream of him waiting for us, walking through the door and finding no one there and calling. Over and over I wake myself with a jump and I see that there is still no sign. Until there is. The nose of the ferry points its way into the corner of the window. There is a second when I am not sure, the same way that there always is. But then I see it and I know he is there. The whole boat is smaller than a toy from here. It is bright against the muddy blackness of Howth. I go and wake her.

'He is coming,' I say.

'What? What time is it?'

'Twenty past seven.'

'It'll be another half hour,' she says. She rolls over onto her back and closes her eyes again.

'The boat has gone past already. We have to go.'

She says nothing for a second. I wonder if she has fallen asleep again.

'If we weren't there he would just get the train home,' she says. 'He would know what to do. It's not like he has forgotten where he lives.'

'We have to go,' I say again. I go and get dressed.

★

I think she drives slowly to annoy me. There is no traffic. When we are stopped at a light that doesn't want to change, I say it to her.

'Why won't you go?'

'Because it's still red.'

'There's nobody around. You can see.'

'You can't even bloody drive.'

'Neither can you. Hardly. No test.' I want to take it back as I say it.

'Don't start with that,' she says after a moment.

'OK,' I say and then she laughs. We both do.

★

Down at the port, the ferry is in. Its front is open like a shark's mouth. The lorries are coming off, groaning and sighing like they are waking up. She waits in the car and I go and stand at the railing looking down into the corridor. In the orange light of the morning it feels like a place for a holiday. But the crowd facing me look angry and lost. They are pushing trolleys that won't go straight and dragging bags that are too big. I hear the accents. The English children with Irish parents that don't fit them. The small Welsh men who laugh together in voices that are too loud for the morning.

And then I see him. In among everybody else, he looks normal. There is nothing that says he is anybody different. A man in a jacket and a tie.

Taller than most people, but not everybody. He looks quiet when he's on his own, but that isn't him. It's just something that I know. He smiles when he sees me. I duck under the railing and walk to him.

'There you are,' he says and pulls me against him for a moment. Not too much, just long enough. He smells tired. 'Where is she?' he asks.

'At the car.'

'How is she?'

I shrug. 'Fine,' I say. 'Normal.'

'So not that fine.'

'She's all right.'

I get in the back as he gets in the front. He leans over and kisses her. She hardly looks at him. It makes me want to hit the back of her seat.

'How have you been?' he asks her.

'How have *you* been?' she says back at him and now she turns.

'I've been OK. It was very calm coming over.'

'Well, that's one good thing.' She starts the car and crunches it into first gear.

'Do you want to go for breakfast or something, maybe? To the hotel?'

'I do,' I say.

'No,' she says. 'Not today.'

'Why not?' I ask her.

'Because,' she says.

'That's not a reason.'

'Leave it,' he says. The rest of the way home none of us says anything.

He goes to bed when we get in. She stays in the kitchen drinking coffee. She makes toast and tea for me. We have breakfast together. Outside I can see that the sun is shining. I know that she'll put me out after this. But I don't want to go. I want to stay inside and watch television. Put on the racing and watch it with him when he comes down.

'It's a nice day,' she says. I know that is going to be the start of it. I don't wait to be told. I get up and leave. I slam the back door behind me, knowing that I have shown her. But after a moment I realise that all I have done is go outside. And outside I have nothing to do.

Two

At eleven o'clock I am with Brian at the bottom of his garden. We are lying in the long grass under the apple trees. We are both smoking cigarettes that he has taken from Pilar. She has a suitcase full of them under her bed. He goes in when she's not there and robs packets of them. She says nothing because he knows things she doesn't want him to. He has a telescope propped on a log aimed at her room. We think she is in the shower and is about to come back in. I take a drag off the cigarette. I hold the smoke in my mouth and then inhale. The smell is like cigars. It hurts but I don't cough.

'These things are rough,' I say.

'Yeah. She ran out of Lucky Strike. I liked them better. These are Spanish ones. Black.'

'Why won't your parents get an Irish girl? With Irish cigarettes?'

'Because Spanish ones are cheaper. And nicer.'

'Let me look,' I say.

'She's not there. I'll give it to you if she comes back.'

'You swear?'

'Yeah.'

For a moment I think about what I would see if I pointed the telescope at our house. If there could be something good that I wouldn't expect.

'There she is,' he says. 'And she is wearing nothing.'

'Let me see.'

'Jesus, I can see everything. The body on this girl.'

'Give. Give.'

He laughs and rolls out of the way. When I look, there is nothing there. I can see the glass of her window, the ceiling of her room, but not her.

'She's gone,' I say.

'Really? She was there a second ago. In the nude. You want to see her. She's a fine thing.'

I know that these words come to him easy because of his brothers. He has heard all of this before. But he doesn't even know what he is talking about.

'She was never there, was she?' I say then.

'I swear she was,' he says and he laughs.

'You're a pain.'

'She was. I saw everything.'

I stub the cigarette out in the grass and stand up. 'You saw nothing,' I say.

'Where are you going?'

'I'm getting the bike and I'm going up to the village.'

'Why are you going now? Do you not want to see?'

I jump the wall. When I'm halfway up my garden, he catches up. He is talking about her as he arrives – what he saw, what was big and what was small and what was round. I don't know what he is talking about. Well, I do but I don't. And I know he doesn't either.

'She wasn't there,' I say again.

'I can't believe you missed it. I'm going to tell everybody about this. It was just beautiful.'

'I don't believe you.'

He stops and grabs me by the arm. He looks me in the eye.

'I'm not messing with you here. We can go back if you want and look again, but she was up there. I don't know why you won't believe me.'

I look for something in him, some shadow to let me know if he is lying. But his face is empty.

'What did you see?' I ask.

'She was wearing nothing,' he says. 'I saw everything.'

★

They are not bad that evening. It is quiet over dinner and then afterwards in the living room watching telly. None of us says much. But we say enough for it to be almost normal. I think maybe it is going to be all right this time. But later on when I'm in bed I hear the noise coming up. It echoes through the hall, into the landing and under the door of my room. There is the same moment of doubt that there always is at first. That maybe it is the television or him sneezing or a chair being moved. But then I hear the tone and I can't escape from it. Never the words. Just the tone and that's enough. The anger in both of them is there. It seeps in and poisons me. I put the radio to my ear and my head under the pillow. I blot it out. All I can hear is the music, some old song that I don't even like. But I remember listening to it before all this, when I was happy and everything was better. I think I remember that.

★

I spend the afternoon with him on the Sunday. We go to a stupid film and then a Chinese restaurant. She has told us that she has work to get done. But I know she doesn't do anything at the weekends. We have the same thing as always in the restaurant. The guy gives us a third dessert for nothing. We talk about the film. When he gives out I join in, relieved that he didn't like it. Happy that he wouldn't lie to save my feelings. We walk down to the port. He rings her from a public phone to say goodbye. I stand outside the phone box. At the end he puts her on to me.

'Do you want me to come down and get you?' she asks.

'I can take the train.'

'Do you have money?'

'I can get it from him,' I tell her.

'Get it now,' she says. 'While I'm on.'

'I will. I will.'

'Now.'

It's the kind of thing she does. I open the door of the phone box and ask him for the fare. He goes to his pocket. He pulls out tissues and bits of paper. With his other hand he picks out coins and gives them to me. A mix of English and Irish. When I have enough I nod, but he keeps going.

'I have it,' I say into the phone.

'Come straight back,' she says. 'Don't go anywhere.'

He is smiling at me as he continues to put coins into my hand. I laugh.

'Do you hear?' she says then.

'OK. Yeah. God.'

I hang up and we walk to the office. He goes in and buys the ticket, bending to talk under the hatch. When he comes out we go to the barrier.

'I'll see you next week,' he says. 'Mind her. Be good and all.'

'I am. I always am.'

'I don't know about that.'

'Most of the time anyway.'

'Fair enough,' he says. He looks over his shoulder at the crowd moving along the corridor. I can see he wants to be a part of it. Then he turns back to me. 'Maybe sometime soon you would come with me.'

'Where? Over there?'

'Maybe. Would you like to?'

'Yeah. Sure.'

'I would be working during the day. But we could work something out. Take a bit of time off. Could be fun.'

'That would be cool.'

'I'll talk to her about it,' he says. 'See you soon.' He hugs me quickly and kisses the top of my head. Then he is gone. I am still waiting there when he reaches the end of the corridor. He turns and waves back in my direction. But I know that he can't see me. It is just something that he has always done.

Three

Near the bottom of the garden there is a half-built wall. The old lad who had the place before us was going to put up a greenhouse, but he died. Just one wall was left standing. It looks stupid, there in the middle of the lawn. Brian is off somewhere with his family. I'm bored. The sun won't shine properly. The sky has been grey all day, as if at any moment it is going to rain. But it doesn't rain and I stay out there.

It starts as nothing at all. An idea that turns up from nowhere. I give the wall a couple of kicks and nothing happens. Then I get a rock from the edge of a flowerbed. I can just about carry it, but it's a good shape. It sits well between my hands. I raise it as high as I can and throw it against the wall. A puff of dust. I think I can see the wall shudder for a moment. Afterwards I'm not so sure. The rock has taken a lump out of one of the blocks in the wall. I pick it up again, with both hands, and this time get it over my head. I aim for the same place. This time I am certain that the whole wall shakes. I get in close and see that a crack is spreading across the top right corner. It doesn't follow the edges of the blocks. It is just its own thing. Something that I have made. I kick at the wall above that crack and I can feel it move. I lift the rock a third time. With more strength than before, I hop it off the weakest point. It seems to happen slowly. A huge chunk crashes to the ground. A cloud of dust rises and catches in my throat. It makes me cough but I'm laughing too. Now I know I can do it all. The whole thing is coming down.

It takes a couple of hours. By the end of it I'm kicking the last blocks to try and loosen them. Then I smash them with the rock. The wall lies in rubble. My hands are red and starting to blister. I stand at the bottom of the garden and look up at the house. I see it differently now without the wall in the way. I go to the top of the garden and realise that they will be able to see more of what I'm doing without the wall there. But I don't let myself worry about that. If I can knock one wall then surely I could knock a house. Leave me alone for a week or two and I could take the school apart. A pile of rubble waiting for everybody in September. I could go to London and work on the sites. It all seems possible.

Inside I find her in the dining room. She is working on a paper. But she comes without complaining when I say I have something to show her. I take her into the kitchen and lead her to the window.

'Now,' I say.

'What am I looking for?' she says.

'Just wait. Does nothing seem different?'

She stares down the garden. I watch her eyes flick from top to bottom, left to right, then stop. Her gaze fixes.

'Where's the wall?' she says, pointing. I laugh. 'What did you do?' she asks.

'I knocked it down.'

'Why?' She turns and opens the back door and walks quickly down the garden. I follow her.

'You said I could,' I say to her back.

'When? When did I say that?'

'When we came here. You said that the wall was stupid looking and we would have to get someone to get rid of it. And I said I could do it. And you said that would be great. You both did.'

'I don't remember that.'

'You said it.'

'OK,' she says. 'OK. Maybe I did. But you should have asked.'

'You said I could do it.'

We are standing now above what is left. She looks at the rubble.

'How are we going to get rid of all this stuff? We'll have to get a guy with a skip and a barrow to take it away. Did you think about that?'

'I will get rid of it,' I say.

'How? Where?'

'At the bottom. Along the wall. It's all weeds anyhow. I'll carry it all down there. There won't be anything left.'

'OK,' she says after a moment. Then she shakes her head and goes back up to the house. I stay where I am. I don't want to go inside now. She stops and looks back at me.

'Was it fun?' she asks. I am not sure what to say.

'It was all right,' I say.

'You must have done it very quickly. What did you use?'

'A rock.'

She laughs then. 'Very creative.'

'I think so,' I say.

She walks back towards me. She seems different now. I thought she was annoyed but there is something else. She stands beside me and touches my face. I let her do it.

'This isn't because of the London thing?' she asks then.

'No. What do you mean?'

'I mean because I wouldn't let you go.'

'No,' I say. I'm fed up now. 'No. That is nothing to do with anything. You told me I could do this.'

'I know,' she says. 'It's just he wouldn't be able to look after you properly during the day. Over there.'

'I can look after myself.'

'I know you can. But it's different in England.'

'I know what it's like. I'd be fine. Why are we talking about this? I just wanted to show you what I'd done. I don't want to talk about this again.'

'I just hope you know I'm not trying to spoil your fun.'

'You keep saying that,' I shout at her. 'You keep saying the same bloody thing but that's all you ever do.'

'I don't,' she says. 'There are things you don't understand.'

'What things? Tell me.'

We stand close, staring at each other. I hope she is going to say something. I hope that she is angry enough to tell me. But as I look at her I see that she is not angry at all. She just looks tired. Right then I really want to hug her. If she moved towards me, if she said anything now, I would do it. But she doesn't. She turns away and walks back up the garden to the house.

Four

Out in the cul-de-sac, Brian and I sit with the others in a circle. One of them, some new guy who I think might be an idiot, is telling them about where he's going in America next week. The States, he says, and it sounds wrong to me.

'We'll stay in New York for a few days and then go to LA and then Chicago and Hollywood.'

Brian laughs and I am glad. He hears it too.

'What's funny?' the guy says. Robert is his name.

'Are these just the places you've heard of?' I say. 'Names that you got off the telly?'

'What do you mean? I'm going next week.'

'To where?'

'To New York and Chicago and LA.'

'That's not what you said before.'

'It is.'

'It's not,' I say. 'You said them in the wrong order. You forgot Hollywood. I think you're making it up.' I'm not worried. He's new and even if the others joined in, Brian and I would still be OK. There is a girl there, someone's sister. She is watching Robert now.

'What order are you talking about?' he says. 'Do you want me to go and get the tickets? I can get them now and show you.' He stands up.

'Great,' I say. 'Show everybody.' There is a flash of doubt across his face. I see it because I'm looking straight at him. I'm still lying on the ground and he is standing above me. I think for a second that he is going to kick me in the head. Just lose his cool and freak out. He doesn't know it, but I'm ready for him. When he turns and walks away I'm almost disappointed.

'He's showing off,' Brian says to the others. 'He's not going anywhere.'

'I think he is,' the girl says. 'He's been there before.'

'How do you know?' I ask.

'He showed me photos.'

'Of what?'

'I don't know. Restaurants and things. Beaches in California. It was America.'

'What, were there flags?'

She shakes her head and looks away. Then she speaks again. 'You two are just being mean for nothing. You're picking on him because he's new.'

'No,' I say, trying to see if it is true. 'We're picking on him because he's lying.' I smile at her, trying to make her see. Trying to make her like me.

'Do you fancy him or something?' Brian says.

'I hate you, Brian Miller,' she says. 'You're a pig.'

Brian laughs but I look at the ground. The Robert guy is coming back. There is nothing in his hands.

'Let's see,' Brian calls. 'Where are they?'

'My mother won't let me bring them out to you,' Robert says. 'But if you want she says to come over to the house and she'll show you.' A couple of the others laugh and I don't know what it means.

'That's crap,' I say. 'You're only saying that because you think we won't go.'

'Come on then,' he says. He takes a few steps back towards his house and then waits. 'Come on.'

'I'm not going to his house,' Brian says to me, standing up. He stretches as if he is more bored than he has ever been before. 'Do you want to go for a smoke in the garden?'

'Sure,' I say. The others are watching us as we get up.

'You're not going?' the girl says. 'You're not going to go and prove that he's lying?'

'We don't need to,' Brian says. 'Where are the tickets? He said he'd get them. I'm not going to go up to his house. I don't know what he's got up there, but I'm not going. He's a messer. He's talking shit.'

'You're just jealous,' she says. She is looking at me as she speaks.

'Of what?' I say. 'Of what?'

'Of me,' Robert says. 'I'm going away next week and you're not. You're trying to make out that I'm lying because you're jealous. Because you're not going anywhere. You'll be stuck here the same way you always are.'

'Who are you? How do you know anything about me?'

'I know all about you,' he says. He has stopped moving and is looking straight at me.

'Actually,' I say, walking towards him, 'I'm going to London next week.' I don't look back to Brian.

'No, you're not,' Robert says.

'Yeah, I am. With my father. He works there and I'm going for the week to stay with him.' I'm standing in his space now. If he says the wrong thing, I'll let it happen.

'London's nothing,' he says. 'It's only England.'

I smile at that. Then I turn away and Brian and I leave. Robert is shouting after me. But I've won because the last thing he said was stupid. Everybody will have known that.

'Are you really going away?' Brian asks when we're across the road.

'I think so. I don't know for sure. I just wanted to shut him up.'

'Well, you did that.'

'Not really. He's still talking.'

'You annoyed him anyway and that's even better.' We both laugh. 'And if you don't go it doesn't matter anyway. Nobody's going to remember.'

'No,' I say. 'They won't.'

Five

On the Tuesday she is away for the day at a conference. She has arranged with Brian's mother that I will have lunch with them. She asks me can I mow the lawn and I say yes. She doesn't talk about money but I think she will give me something. She always does for garden stuff. Weeding and raking leaves and that.

'Get it done before lunch,' she says before she leaves. 'It may rain later. And then you can relax in the afternoon.'

'I'd rather do it later,' I say. Not because it's true – just for something to say. To see what she'll do.

'Are you trying to annoy me?' she asks.

'Yes,' I say after a second and she laughs.

'I don't have time to be annoyed,' she says. 'Be good. See you later.'

She kisses me before I can get away. As I'm wiping her perfume off my face, she goes. I turn on the television but there is nothing to watch. I go upstairs and look through their room for anything that might be interesting. There is nothing there. After a while I go out. The sun is shining now. I don't mind doing the grass. I like the machine. The noise of it and the power. Every time he took it out he used to tell me about people who lost fingers trying to unblock it when it was on. 'You'd want to be pretty stupid,' I said to him the last time. 'That's why I'm telling you,' he said.

It is cooler in the shed. The dark musty smell of wood and oil and petrol that I remember from forever. I get down on my hands and knees and take the cap off the lawnmower. I look in and see the broken reflection of my eye in the liquid. Only half full. I get the plastic can and attach the spout to it. I fill the machine, listening to the happy glugging sound until it splashes back. Some of it spills across the engine. Not much but enough to make me wait for a couple of minutes before starting it. There is petrol on my hand, cold as it evaporates. I hold my fist to my nose and sniff. I love it. I don't know what it reminds me of, but it seems to be something good.

I push back the door of the shed and look across the empty patio. I walk back out into the sunshine and stare through the kitchen window to the drive at the front of the house. The car is definitely gone. She is not there. I feel something in my stomach, like sickness. There is something that I am afraid I know I will do.

I go back into the shed and kneel down again. I take the spout off the can and lift it to my face. I put my nose to the hole and breathe in. A wave of happiness washes over me. A warmth spreads through me as I breathe out and listen. I know I'm not supposed to do this, but I don't know why. I didn't know it would be like this. So relaxed. One more time and there's a noise in my ear. I can taste the petrol now in my mouth. This beautiful smell is everywhere about me. I breathe in again, sniffing deep. I stay there for not very long, in and out. When I look up the shed has turned into something else. It is the place I know best in the world. It looks to me now as if it has grown together the way I see it. I couldn't change it. I reach out to touch the shears that sit upside down on a shelf. All that I can see is the shears. There is nothing else now. Shears, I try to say, but it sounds wrong. Shears, I say again and the shed laughs with me. Out, out now into the daylight to the garden away from my home here in the shed. Goodbye, I say, and there is a chorus of goodbyes from everything in there. A pile of coal sings to me.

Out in the sunshine I can't see anything. Just whiteness. Then in a second the colour comes. The birds sing together as I walk out. Then they line up on a phone wire above the garden. They are all black and they whistle together. We know, they say. We know about you. Don't tell anyone, I say to them. We never tell, they sing and I sing it with them as I walk down the garden. The grass is made of dots that I've never seen before, a sea of dots. But then I look up and the sky is the same. I look at the bark of the tree in the middle of the lawn and it is the same. I look at the palm of my hand and now I know. I am made of these dots, the same pattern as everything else. As everybody else. I just never saw it before. All these things I never knew. We are all the same, I say to the blackbirds, and they sing it back to me. It changes then. He is coming, they say. He is coming. They chant it at me over and over. And when I look down the garden to where the wall used to be, my father is standing on a conveyer belt. He is chugging along towards me in time as the birds chant, He is coming, he is coming. I didn't do anything, I say when he's still too far away to hear. But then I see that he has gone.

The birds' chanting fades away. I look at my hand again and the dots are disappearing. I open and close my palm, watching as they go. I laugh to myself as I walk back up to the shed. That was something, I say out loud. I hear my voice as if it belongs to someone else. I get the mower out, wheel it to edge of the lawn and pull the chord. It starts first time, chugging slowly for a second before building into its usual roar.

★

In Brian's kitchen his mother is frying chips in a pan. Brian and I are eating bread. He is telling me about some soccer school he wants to go to in August. He says I should do it too. He says that we could meet other people there. I'm not sure if I want to.

'These other people,' I say to him, 'who are they going to be?'

'I don't know. People our age.'

'Just boys?'

'Yes,' his mother says.

'Is it?' he asks.

'Yeah.'

'I thought it was both,' he says.

'That one was full,' she says, putting a plate in front of each of us. 'Boys only, I'm afraid.' She sits at the table and lights a cigarette.

'Well, anyway. I think we should.'

'Can you smell petrol?' she asks then out of nowhere. I hold my breath.

'No,' Brian says. He sniffs the air. 'Or maybe.'

'That's me,' I say then. The two of them stare. I don't have time to think. But I know it is better to say something.

'I was cutting the grass before. I spilt petrol on my hands when I was filling the mower. It splashed all over the place.'

'You could have told me before I lit this,' she says, waving the cigarette in the air. 'You're a bloody fire hazard. Get into the bathroom and wash yourself, will you?'

'I did already.'

'Well do it again. Please. I don't want to have to explain to your mother that I burnt you to death.'

'She wouldn't mind,' I say and she laughs.

In the bathroom I see that there's a red ring around my nose. Not too clear. You mightn't notice if you weren't looking for it. I wash my face with soap and hot water but it seems to make it worse. I go back into the kitchen and keep my head down.

'I can still smell it,' his mother says after a moment. She has stubbed the cigarette out in the ashtray and has stood up. 'What happened?' she asks then. 'Were you swimming in it?'

'No,' I say, too loud, too hard. She is above me looking down. 'No,' I say again, quieter this time.

'I'm only messing with you,' she says as she walks behind my chair. She clips me across the back of the head. When I look up, she is smiling at me. I try to smile back but I don't feel it.

Six

That night in my room, I am looking at the ceiling. She has just gone to bed. The door of her room is closed. I sit up and lean against the wall, looking out across the bay. The lights along the coast road in Clontarf are orange. The ones on the hill of Howth straight across from here are yellow and white. At the end there is a lighthouse. It flashes three times, then nothing for fifteen seconds, then three flashes again.

When I was younger I wanted to be the lighthouse man. The man at the end of the land on his own with the birds. Then my father told me that they were all automatic now. He said that the light just spins without anyone's help. But still I can believe that the man is there. If I don't think about it, I can feel that he is signalling for me. And I think if I watch for long enough, he will make a mistake. One flash too few. Five seconds too long. Then I will know that he is there. Not really, but real enough.

Out my window I can see the roof of the shed. If I sat on the window sill and jumped over to the right I could land on it. Then I could go down the drainpipe and let myself in. I could lie on the floor in the coal with the can to my face for hours. Just stay there and let my mind drift. I could do it. I would be back in the morning before she knew. But how would I get up to my room? The back door would be locked. I could never reach the window.

Then it comes to me. I could go downstairs now. I could wait in the kitchen to see if she heard me. If she came down I could say I needed milk. I could let myself out and wait on the patio. If she came I could say I heard a sound. I could open the door of the shed and wait. Then when I knew she hadn't heard me, I could go in. I could do it. The part of me that feels happiest tells me that I can do it.

I lie back on the bed and look at the ceiling. In the glass of the picture on the wall, I see the flash of the lighthouse. Ten more goes, I think to myself. If I'm still awake after the three flashes have gone ten times, then I'll go downstairs. I begin to count in the darkness. At eight I'm as awake as I was when I started. Then one, two, three.

Wait. One, two, three again. Now I know there is no way around it. I'll never sleep if I don't at least start to try. It is still exciting but there is sadness in me now. I just want to be down there with the can in my hand.

I get out of bed and walk across the room. It takes a minute to get through the door without a sound. I float across the landing as light as I can. I stop at the top of the stairs. Her breathing is deep. She is definitely asleep. I go down the stairs, skipping the ones that creak, stepping in the right place on the others. Then I go through the kitchen in the dark where I bang into a chair. It groans in protest, trying to rat me out. I freeze. The sound echoes in my ear. But then nothing else follows. I stand at the back door and wait.

I understand the comfort of before and the fear of after. I could go back up now to bed and get in and fall asleep straight away. It seems like a good idea but I know it won't happen. If I have come this far I may as well go the rest of the way. I turn the key in the lock and the sound explodes in the darkness. I wait again, then turn the handle. I get out and close the door behind me.

The air on the patio is cool. The ground under my bare feet is damp. I go down the garden to look up at her room. I'm surprised by how wet the grass is. Her room is in darkness. I wait for a minute, looking up at the house and listening. The only sound outside is of traffic on the main road. Dogs barking now and then. Sometimes a single car comes past our house. But nothing sounds unusual.

I am walking towards the shed door when the light in the kitchen goes on. The whole world is different in that yellow brightness. I move back into the dark as quick as I can. But then I see her coming towards the window. I stand still. She takes a glass out of one of the presses and runs the cold tap. Her eyes are barely open and her hair is messy. She stands in the window and drinks one glass down. Then she refills it. She leans on the sink and looks out the window in my direction, yawning. I cannot move. She stays there staring straight at me and I do not move. I'm so close to her but I know that I'm standing in the darkness. If she had heard something she would have come out by now. She would be doing something more than just drinking water and staring at nothing. After a couple of minutes she picks up the glass and turns away. A second later, the light goes out.

I stay where I am, in the same position, and wait. I can't feel my feet any more. My chest hurts from holding my breath too much. I give her what feels like ten minutes and then go to the back door. As I turn the handle, I think that she might have turned the key before going back up. But when I push, the door swings open. I lock it behind me, make my way through the kitchen and back up the stairs. The bedside light in her room is on. I cross the landing. Outside the bathroom a floorboard creaks.

'Danny?' she says from her room.

'Yeah?'

'You OK?'

'Just going to the toilet.' I go into the bathroom and realise that I do want to pee. When I come out and I'm just at the door of my room, she calls out, 'Goodnight.'

'Goodnight,' I say back to her. In my room I sit looking out across the bay until my heart slows down enough to let me sleep.

Seven

The next weekend he comes on the ferry into Dublin Port so we don't go to meet him. I wake on the Saturday and know that he is home. I go into their room but no one is there. The two of them are sitting at the table in the kitchen saying nothing when I walk in.

'Hello,' I say.

'Hi.'

Something is not right here.

'How was it coming across?' I ask anyway.

'Fine. It was fine.' He stands up and stretches, then puts the kettle on. She is looking straight ahead. She hasn't turned towards me since I have come in.

'Now,' he says.

'Now what?' I say, jokey. I have done it before. I have made things better by sounding happy and normal.

'Your mother tells me you haven't been great this week.'

I look at her but still she won't turn. 'What does that mean?'

'Rude. Unhelpful. She says you've hardly been talking to her.'

'It's true,' she says, looking at me now. 'You know it's true.'

'No,' I say. 'I don't think it is.'

'It's not easy for her,' he says. 'During the week. You have to help. You have to do what you are told.'

'That is not the problem,' she says.

'I thought that's what you said …'

'No. It's the sulking. The moods. I just can't bear it.'

'Why didn't you say it to me then?' I ask her.

'I did.'

'No, you didn't.'

'I asked you over and over if there was something wrong. You kept saying no.'

'Is there?' he says. 'Is there something wrong?'

'No,' I say.

'Then for Christ's sake will you just cheer up and do what you're supposed to do,' he says.

I am staring at her. She looks at me once, turns away and then looks back.

'What?' she says.

'Nothing. Nothing.'

'I think it's better that you don't come to London at the moment,' he says. 'You need to start being a bit more mature before you come.'

'That was already decided,' I say. 'Or I thought it was.'

'Well, not now,' he says. 'If you start behaving right, we might consider it for later on. The end of the summer, maybe.'

Out of nowhere she hits the table and curses. The two of us watch in silence as she stands up. She walks out of the room, shaking her head and muttering. 'Enough,' I hear her say.

'Would you please, please be good to her?' he says in a tired voice after she has gone.

'I am. I swear to you, I am.'

'She doesn't seem to think so,' he says.

'Why don't you try it, then? See what it's like,' I say. There is no delay. The next thing he is standing beside me with a finger in my face.

'Don't talk like that,' he says. 'You do not have the right to talk like that.'

If I say the wrong thing now I think he might hit me. So I don't speak. He leaves without saying anything else and follows her into the living room. The door slams. I hear him starting to talk to her. I grab a yoghurt and some bread and go out into the garden. After I have eaten, I start to carry the rubble down to the patch of weeds at the back wall.

★

The next week I am lying in the grass under the trees with a rag to my face. She is off somewhere. It doesn't matter now that I can't remember where it is. All that I am sure of is that she will be gone all day. The trees give me shade from the sun that is shining above. In the light that comes through the branches, I am watching things happen to the house. The upstairs windows are its eyes. The downstairs dining room is its mouth. It is a big swaying head. And if it wasn't for the birds I would be freaking out. They are singing again. The house is sad, they are saying. Go to it. I don't want to, I say. Then I see that the house is starting to cry. Aww, say the birds. Aww. Go to it. Go to him. Is it a him? Maybe I should go because I can see that the house needs to be comforted.

I stand up and walk through the garden. But then I see that the flowers near the washing line are crying too. No, I say. It's all right. Everything is OK. But they won't stop. The sound upsets me. I bend down. One by one I kiss the flowers. When I do, they smile at me. By the time I have finished, they are singing too. It is all so beautiful and happy. And then I remember I have to get to the house. It is the last thing I need to do. Then everything will be fine.

When I look up the garden I see Brian standing there, staring at me. I turn back to the flowers. Do you think that is him? I ask them. It's Brian, they say. Brian. I'm surprised they know him. I walk towards him. He says something that sounds backwards to me. I smile at him and laugh to let him know that I'm OK. I'm worried now. He speaks again and I don't understand.

'Hmm?' I say.

'Are you all right?' he says then, suddenly clear.

'I'm fine, yeah.' My voice sounds strange in my ears. Slow and deep. Very loud.

'What were you doing there? With the flowers?'

'Smelling them. I was smelling them.'

'What for?'

I try to be normal. 'Because I want to. I don't have to tell you why. What has it got to do with you?'

He is staring at me now.

'Just seems weird to me,' he says. 'Are you sure you're all right? You look different.'

'I'm fine,' I say. 'What do you want anyway?'

'Do you want to come with me to the pool? The slide is open.'

'When?'

'Now. My mother is going to drive us.'

'I can't,' I say. 'I've got to mind the house.'

'Your mother said it would be fine. She just talked to mine earlier. She said she wanted you to go. It'll be good. Come on.'

'I'm not going.'

'Why?'

'Because you are being a dick. I don't want to go. I'm going to stay here and look after myself.'

'What's wrong with you?' he asks.

'Nothing. What's wrong with you?'

He watches me for a second then turns away. I watch him as he gets to the wall beside the house and jumps it. I hear the back door of his house slam. Then I go inside. In the bathroom I wash my face and brush my teeth. My skin is red around my nose and mouth. I know not to rub at it and that it will fade soon. When I'm coming back downstairs, the doorbell rings. I look out the window. I see Brian's mother's car parked in front of our gate. Brian is sitting in the front seat. I make my way down and open the door.

'Not in the mood for swimming?' she says. 'Is everything all right?'

'No. It's grand,' I say. I don't want to talk to her for too long.

'Ah, come on. Go and get your togs. Keep this miserable guy company.' She jerks her thumb towards the car at the gate. When I look, Brian is staring straight ahead.

'Thanks, but I don't really feel like it. I'll be fine here.'

'Your mother said you would love to. She thought you would be glad to get away from the house.'

'Not today,' I say. 'I have some stuff to do.'

'What stuff?'

'Just things.' What will it take to get rid of her?

She nods and smiles. 'OK,' she says. 'Well, I tried.'

'Thanks very much.'

'See you later. Come in if you need anything to eat. Any time.'

'I will,' I say, thinking that is the end of it. Before I know what is happening, she leans forward and puts an arm around me. She kisses the side of my face quickly. I don't pull away, but I know I don't feel normal. When her face is close to mine I hear her breathe in. Suddenly I feel sick. I stand at the door and watch her go. She starts the car. As she pulls away, Brian looks over and lifts his hand – just for a second.

Eight

As soon as she arrives home, I know that she has heard. She comes into the living room and I know that she knows. I turn the television off. She walks over. As she stands above me, I think for a second that she is going to hit me. She never has before, but this is different. It is all much quieter than I thought it would be. She asks me what I have been doing. The truth falls out of me. I don't want to keep anything back from her.

'Why do you it?' she asks once she has heard. 'Does it feel really good?'

'Yes. I like it. That's why.'

'Do you know it's bad for you?'

I shrug. 'Everything is bad for you,' I say and chance a smile.

'No,' she says. 'This is really bad for you. It could kill you.' She is looking at me now, trying to see if that shocks me. It doesn't. 'Is that what you want?' she asks. 'To kill yourself?'

'No,' I say.

'Then you have to stop. You have to.'

I nod this time.

'What are we going to do?' she says then.

There is a full minute of silence. Then I speak, trying to make her feel better. 'I don't know.'

'We'll have to see what Dad says anyway. But will you stop? Please? Never again?'

'Yes.'

She kneels on the ground in front of me and holds me for a minute. 'Promise me,' she says into my neck.

'I promise you,' I say. And as I hear the words, I know that I mean them.

★

The next morning she is working in the dining room. I go out into the garden, down to the bottom, and jump the wall into Brian's. I start walking up towards his house. Then I see him sitting on the swing. He is looking at a comic that he holds in one hand. I look up to the kitchen window of his house. I see that no one is there.

'Hi,' he says. 'Where have you been?'

I have told myself that I'm going to hit him in the face. But when it comes to it, I can't. I punch him hard in the chest. He falls backwards off the swing.

His feet are tangled in the chain and he can't get up. I kick at him once, not hard, but just enough to scare him.

'I didn't tell her,' he says. 'I didn't say anything, I swear to you.'

'You are not my friend any more. That's it.'

'I'm telling you,' he says. 'Come on, Danny.'

'You're a liar. That's all you are.' I move as if I'm going to kick him again. But I don't want to. He is not trying to fight back. He looks up at me and he just seems lost. I run back down his garden and jump into ours. I hear him calling my name as I go.

I head straight back into the house.

'Everything OK?' she calls as I come through the hall.

'Yeah.'

She comes out and stands in front of me. 'You sure?'

I try to smile at her. 'Definitely.'

'You're a good fellow,' she says, smiling at me.

★

That Friday I can't get to sleep. I sit on the bed watching the lights of cars on the Clontarf Road. I know that she has told him. They have talked more this week on the phone than they normally do. It worries me to think of it. But she hasn't told me what he has said. We haven't talked about it at all since that day. We have just been acting as if everything is normal. They might send me to a doctor or for counselling. They could send me to another school. I don't see why it has to mean anything. It is something that I did that I won't do again. That's all there is to it.

I wake up with my head at the bottom of the bed. I sit up and look out and see that the boat is nearly in. I don't even want to go this time. But then she comes to the door wearing a dressing gown and shoes.

'Got to go,' she says.

We get down quickly enough. They are still trying to get the ferry lined up when we park. I think about waiting in the car with her. But I don't want it to seem different than usual. Maybe he will have forgotten. Or won't think it is that important. I'll know as soon as I see him. The crowd starts to come after ten minutes. It feels like it's the same people every week, but I never recognise anyone. I wait and the crowd begins to thin. Then the last few families and old people come. And then the only people in the corridor are wearing uniforms. I duck under the barrier and go up to one of them.

'Is that everyone?' I ask.

'Yes, son,' the guy says. 'They're all off. Why? Who are you waiting on?'

'My father.'

'Well, he may have missed it. He could be on this evening's ship. Or he could be pissed in a pub in Holyhead.' A couple of the others in uniform laugh at him. He laughs too for a second. Then he seems to change when he looks at me. 'I'm sure he's fine. One of the trains may have broken down. It happens. He'll probably ring you later.' I walk away without saying anything.

'He wasn't on it,' I say to her as I get back into the car.

'What? Are you sure?'

'He just wasn't.'

She looks at me to see if I'm joking.

'Maybe the next one, the guy said.'

'What guy?'

'I don't know. Someone who worked there.'

She leans forward and holds her head in her hands. It takes a minute for me to realise that she is crying. I don't know what to do. I reach over and rub the back of her neck. She lets me hug her. Then she pulls away and laughs as if she is embarrassed.

'We'll be all right if we stick together,' she says. I nod, although I don't really know what she means. 'I need you to be good for me,' she says. And I'll be good to you. I know it's hard for you, but we need each other. And if we look after each other we'll be OK. You know that, don't you? Nothing else matters. Just that.'

'Yeah, I know,' I say.

'I'm sorry,' she says.

'For what?'

'Just all this.' She sits up and starts the car. She backs out of the space and starts driving towards home.

'I'm sorry too,' I say then, maybe too late.

'You have nothing to be sorry about.'

I let things settle down before I ask the question. 'Is he going to come back?'

'Of course he is,' she says. 'He will probably be home later on. I just wish he had phoned first to let us know.'

He rings that night. He says he is sorry. He got called into work and couldn't get in touch. He says he will be back the following weekend. I talk to him quickly, as the money is running out. He says he is sorry he won't be over this week but we'll talk next weekend. 'Because we have things to talk about,' he says. 'Don't we?'

'I think so,' I say, but I'm not sure any more what they are.

★

She goes out to a meeting on the Tuesday. It is the first time she has left me there since she found out about the petrol. Things have been happy between us over the weekend. After his call she seemed to be all right again. She comes to my room and says goodbye when I'm still in bed. She tells me that she has left something for breakfast under the grill.

I get up as soon as she has gone. I have a shower and then go downstairs. It is beautiful outside. I want to be out there but I still haven't talked to Brian. I go out onto the patio to see if there is any sign of him, but he is not around. As I'm going back in to eat, I stop at the door of the shed. I look in. After the glare of the sunshine, there is only darkness. I know I promised her, but I need one last time. I didn't know before I got caught that that would be the end.

I don't let myself think any more about it. I step into the cool shed. When my eyes adjust, I see the mower right in front of me. I can cut the grass after, I think to myself. That will be my payment to put it right. I kneel down and unscrew the cap. I get my nose right in and breathe long and hard, deeper than ever, one breath after another. That wonderful feeling of being the way I'm supposed to be rolls over me. The dots come first behind my eyelids. Then the whining and the start of the music and then nothing.

It hurts me. Slowly I realise that I am in blackness. I am surrounded by faint stars in the distance. None of them are close to me. It is very cold and I am on my own. When I look then I understand that I too am a star. I am barely alight at all. There is a low humming noise that I realise is coming from me. I know that to burn like this hurts me. And I know that this is all there will be until one day I burn out and it will be over. This is where I am now. Stuck. Burning. Alone.

It begins to brighten. The stars disappear. The light comes back. And then I see a face looking down at me.

'Are you all right?' he asks.

'Are you an angel?' I say, reaching out to him.

'No,' Brian says. He looks confused, worried. I am lying on my back in the doorway of the shed, my head on the patio. My arm is hurting. I must have hit it when I fell.

'Are you all right?' he says again.

'I'm fine,' I say, sitting up.

'What happened?' he asks.

'I don't know. I was at the mower and then I saw you.'

'Were you sniffing it?'

'Yeah,' I say. 'But that's it. That's over now.'

'I didn't tell her,' he says then.

'I know. I was wrong,' I say.

I stand up and together we walk

down through the garden. Neither of us says anything. I can smell the grass and feel the sun on my skin.

OPEN DOOR SERIES

SERIES ONE

Sad Song by Vincent Banville

In High Germany by Dermot Bolger

Not Just for Christmas by Roddy Doyle

Maggie's Story by Sheila O'Flanagan

Jesus and Billy Are Off to Barcelona
by Deirdre Purcell

Ripples by Patricia Scanlan

SERIES TWO

No Dress Rehearsal by Marian Keyes

Joe's Wedding by Gareth O'Callaghan

The Comedian by Joseph O'Connor

Second Chance by Patricia Scanlan

Pipe Dreams by Anne Schulman

Old Money, New Money by Peter Sheridan

SERIES THREE

An Accident Waiting to Happen
by Vincent Banville
The Builders by Maeve Binchy
Letter from Chicago by Cathy Kelly
Driving with Daisy by Tom Nestor
It All Adds Up by Margaret Neylon
Has Anyone Here Seen Larry?
by Deirdre Purcell

SERIES FOUR

The Story of Joe Brown by Rose Doyle
Stray Dog by Gareth O'Callaghan
The Smoking Room by Julie Parsons
World Cup Diary by Niall Quinn
Fair-Weather Friend by Patricia Scanlan
The Quiz Master by Michael Scott

SERIES FIVE

Mrs Whippy by Cecelia Ahern

The Underbury Witches by John Connolly

Mad Weekend by Roddy Doyle

Not a Star by Nick Hornby

Secrets by Patricia Scanlan

Behind Closed Doors by Sarah Webb

SERIES SIX

Lighthouse by Chris Binchy

The Second Child by John Boyne

Three's a Crowd by Sheila O'Flanagan

Bullet and the Ark by Peter Sheridan

An Angel at My Back by Mary Stanley

Star Gazing by Kate Thompson